Foreword

The Critter Crew project started the first year that I taught preschool. I spent countless evenings looking for just the right music for the next day's lesson. I scoured every tape, CD, and children's songbook I could get my hands on. I even searched online and in catalogs and pulled out old records. I just couldn't find what I was looking for. Then, about halfway through the school year, it dawned on me: I've been writing music since I was thirteen years old. I could certainly write these songs as well as anybody. And so I began.

This A-to-Z collection of songs and pictures easily teaches kids the sounds of the alphabet! It really works! Kids love the catchy songs and fun animals; parents and teachers love how their kids learn the alphabet sounds so quickly.

I spent the next few months creating the product that I'd been looking for: a collection of fun music with catchy melodies; get-up-and-dance rhythms; and silly, memorable lyrics that would get those alphabet fundamentals right into my students' eager young minds. I sang it all into a microphone in my home studio and became the voice of Melody Lou.

When I began introducing the music in class, my students loved the songs. They begged for their favorites; they even taught them to neighbor kids. They learned the letter sounds quickly and easily and were reading simple words in no time. I was amazed with the results!

The alphabet songs became a core part of my curriculum. It made my job as a teacher much easier. Not only that, but my own toddlers loved the songs and were learning the alphabet sounds just as quickly as my students! I kept thinking: there are a whole lot of young children out there and these alphabet songs would be great for every one of them. Now—many thanks to Building Blocks Press—the songs are available to all with this companion picture book illustrated by Kathy Voerg. I'm sure you agree that Kathy's artwork is delightful. She's captured the spirit of the Critter Crew animals and created a magical boost for kids' imaginations where they can ride the ocean waves with surfing turtles, peek at napping lions in Africa, eat lunch with a vegetarian vulture, and more—all while they learn the alphabet!

To you and your youngsters, I wish you many happy hours with *Critter Crew with Melody Lou: Alphabet Songs*. If you have comments, questions, or suggestions about this product, please send an email to me at cburnett@buildingblockspress.com. I can't wait to hear from you!

—Christine Burnett

Christine Burnett, Author

Christine Burnett is a preschool and piano teacher as well as an award-winning composer. Her musical compositions range from fun and silly educational songs to sacred choral cantatas to violin/piano duets and piano solos. Christine earned a degree in early-childhood education and minored in music at Brigham Young University in Provo, Utah. She lives in Rochester, New York, with her husband Matthew and their four children, Benjamin, Joshua, Anna, and Maria.

Kathy Voerg, Illustrator

Kathy Voerg is an illustrator working and living outside of New York City. She's a graduate of Pratt Institute in Brooklyn, New York, where she majored in illustration. During her career, she has worked on a variety of children's projects including picture books, coloring books, storyboards, and textile design. She also develops characters to be used in advertising and TV shows. If you are interested in seeing more of her work, visit her website at www.KathyVoerg.com.

Praise for Critter Crew with Melody Lou: Alphabet Songs

I love the *Critter Crew Alphabet Songs*! There is nothing like it on the market and it's the best tool I've found to help children learn their phonics. I have a student who has trouble focusing on other learning techniques, but when we sing the *Critter Crew with Melody Lou: Alphabet Songs,* he is mesmerized and able to focus on the songs. They bring out his personality and he learns quickly from the music. I've used the music with about 150 students and many of their parents say the kids sing the songs at home as well. The lyrics and tunes are very memorable and they easily teach kids the alphabet sounds.

—Evelyn Martinez, preschool teacher

Critter Crew with Melody Lou: Alphabet Song is one of the most engaging and captivating resources out there for teaching young children. It is fun, exciting, and developmentally appropriate for early childhood. Parents and teachers will love it as a tool to help their children begin to read!

—Sheryl Mitchell, reading specialist and kindergarten teacher

My 19-month-old grandson was playing in the living room while I was in the kitchen. The "A" song on the *Critter Crew Alphabet Songs* CD had just ended when he got up off the floor and came to me waving his arms, saying, "Ah, ah, ah!" The *Critter Crew* music is teaching him the letter sounds, even as a very young child.

—Sandy Browning, grandmother

I play the songs while the kids eat lunch, and they love it! It's amazing to see how easily the letter sounds come to them—even when they aren't concentrating. It's the power of music.

—Carolyn Overturf, day-care provider

My four-year-old daughter was born with a cleft palate and now she requires weekly speech therapy sessions. When her preschool teacher introduced her to the *Critter Crew* music, my daughter instantly loved the music and characters. She is learning the letter sounds and focusing on pronouncing the words in the songs. (She really needs to practice her pronunciation in order to be understood.) She sings along with all the songs, has memorized several of them, and has decided to learn all the songs and pronounce the words exactly as they are sung on the CD.

—Moana Blietschau, mother

I use the *Critter Crew* music as part of the curriculum in my fine arts preschool. My students love singing the songs and hearing the stories that they tell. I am so glad to have songs to help them learn the sounds that each letter makes. Music is such a powerful way to learn. Many of my parents have also wanted this music to use at home. They like hearing their children sing as much as I do!

—Angela Olson, Kindermusik teacher

My two-year-old daughter loves the *Critter Crew* music. It took her just two months to learn half the letter sounds in the alphabet. I couldn't be more pleased with this music!

—Jennifer Adams, mother

As a teacher of blind preschool-age children, I found the *Critter Crew Alphabet Songs* to be very, very good. My goal was to get the kids to talk; and as they would listen, they began humming—which is the first step to learning to talk. The kids loved listening to the music and eventually began to say the sounds of the letters. I knew they were understanding what they heard because they began laughing more and more as they would listen to the songs. I saw genuine happiness in the children's faces.

—Bob Zancanella, former teacher for the Utah School for the Deaf and Blind

For Grace, Megan, and Kyle

For Benjamin, Joshua, Anna, and Maria
and for Matthew

For Merlin, Kristi, Mom, Dad, and family

Critter Crew
with Melody Lou
Alphabet Songs

Music and Lyrics by Christine Burnett
Illustrations by Kathy Voerg

Published by Building Blocks Press
129 Bremmer St.
Richland, WA 99352
www.buildingblockspress.com

ISBN 13: 978-0-98171-150-8
Library of Congress Control Number: 2008930253

08 09 10 11 12 13   8 7 6 5 4 3 2 1

For information about bulk sales or educational and promotional pricing, please contact
sales@buildingblockspress.com or write to Building Blocks Press, 129 Bremmer St., Richland, Washington 99352

Printed in China

building blocks press

Sing Along

There was an anteater on an anthill,
who said, "Ay, ay, ahh!" (Repeat)
"I want some ants for breakfast,
or lunch, or dinner. Ahh."
(Repeat first lines of stanza.)

Well, the ants, they heard her comin.'
They said, "Ah, ah, ah!" (Repeat)
"We don't want to be her breakfast,
or lunch, or dinner. Ah!"
(Repeat first two lines of stanza.)

Then, the ants, they got an idea.
They said, "Ha, ha, hay!" (Repeat)
"We'll pinch her nose when it comes in.
We'll make her go away."
(Repeat first two lines of stanza.)

When the anteater put her nose in,
she said, "Ah, ah, ay!" (Repeat)
"I won't have those ants for breakfast,
if they treat me in this way."
(Repeat first two lines of stanza.)

Aa

Track
2

Sing Along

"Buzz, buzz," said the bee
as he buzzed from tree to tree.
(Repeat twice.)
"I like b.......buzzing."

"Brr, brr," said the bee
as he blew in the breeze.
(Repeat twice.)
"I don't like this b.......breeze."

"Bounce, bounce," said the bee
as he bounced from tree to tree.
(Repeat twice.)
"I will bounce through this
b.......breeze."

Bb

Track
3

Sing Along

The cat went climbing up the clock
(Repeat twice)
to see what she could see.
"I see a ceiling fan. See, see, see." (Repeat)

The cat curled up on top that clock
(Repeat twice)
to sleep, no sound to hear. But
"K, k," she heard the clock. "K, k, k." (Repeat)

The cat went climbing down the clock
(Repeat twice)
to smell what she could smell.
Cake, caramel, candy canes, c.....cookies.
(Repeat)

Just then the clock tic-toc, tic-tocked
(Repeat twice)
and cook called, "Kitty cat!
Come, come, come eat your cake.
c.....come!" (Repeat)

Track
4

Dd

Sing Along

Dee was a dog who
could dribble.
He d......dribbled.
In the dark at the park
he'd dribble and bark.
He d......dribbled.

Then on the next
day he drooped.
He d......drooped.
In the goop of his soup,
he said, "I'm kaput."
He d......drooped.

And on the next day
he drooled.
He d......drooled.
In the gool of his pool
he felt rather cool.
He d......drooled.

Dee, d......, my dog.
D......, he dribbled,
he drooped, he drooled.

Track
5

Sing Along

There was an elephant
who liked to eat, eat, eat, e......eat
everything, oh, everything, e.....everything.

She'd eat eggs and extra envelopes. She ate an engine from a train. That exit sign was excellent, or so she did explain.

(Repeat first stanza.)

She'd eat elevators, unoccupied. She ate the elm tree just last spring. She enjoyed that tall electric pole, but admits it was extreme.

(Repeat first stanza.)

Ee

Ff

Sing Along

"F, F," said the frog as he frolicked on the log. (Repeat twice)
"I'm a fantastic fine little frog."

"F, F," said the fly as he flew in the sky. (Repeat twice)
"I'm a fantastic fine little fly."

"F, F," said the fish as he floundered in the dish. (Repeat twice)
"I'm a fantastic fine little fish."

"F, F," said the flamingo as she flitted and mingled. (Repeat twice)
"I'm a fantastic fine flamingo."

Gg

Hh

Track
9

Sing Along

I have an iguana, an iguana named Iggy.
I invented an igloo for him to live in.
It wasn't of ice, didn't smell very nice,
but it was white.

I have an iguana, an iguana named Iggy.
He started to itch in that igloo he lived in.
It wasn't of ice, didn't smell very nice,
but it was white.

(In wild iguanas inhabit the
trees. I think Iggy likes living in
something more green.)

I have an iguana, an iguana named Iggy.
Who lives in a tree!

Ii

Track 10

Jj

Sing Along

Some jays I know
like to jump, jump, jump,
jump, jump, jump. (Repeat)
'Cause jumping makes them
jolly, j.....jolly. (Repeat)

Some jays I know
like to jog, jog, jog,
jog, jog, jog. (Repeat)
'Cause jogging makes them
jolly, j.....jolly. (Repeat)

Some jays I know
like to joke, joke, joke,
joke, joke, joke. (Repeat)
'Cause joking makes them
jolly, j......jolly. (Repeat)

Some jays I know like to
juggle, juggle, juggle, juggle,
juggle, juggle. (Repeat)
'Cause juggling makes them
jolly, j......jolly. (Repeat)

Track 11

Sing Along

King Kay, king kangaroo,
King of the
Kicking Kangaroos
(Repeat)

King Kay kissed his
kitty and sneezed.
"Kerchoo, k......kerchoo!"
(Repeat)

Sing Along

Little ladybug, little ladybug
looked at the lion. (Repeat)
He licked his lazy lips;
he lifted half an eyelid.
Little ladybug, little ladybug
looked at the lion.

Little ladybug, little ladybug
leaned on the lion. (Repeat)
He licked his lazy lips;
he lifted half an eyelid.
Little ladybug, little ladybug
leaned on the lion.

Little ladybug, little ladybug
laughed at the lion. (Repeat)
He licked his lazy lips;
he lifted half an eyelid.
Little ladybug, little ladybug
laughed at the lion.

Lucky ladybug!

Track
13

Mm

Sing Along

Mischievous monkeys munch, munch, munch on their lunch, on their lunch. (Repeat)

They munch on macaroni.
They munch, munch, munch, munch, munch.

They munch on marvelous melons.
They munch, munch, munch, munch, munch, munch, munch, munch, munch, munch, munch. Mmm, mmm, mmm.

Nn

Sing Along

No nightingale I know needs nails.
N.......no.
None in the wild and none in a pen,
No nightingale I know needs nails.

A nightingale needs a nice nest,
Nice for her little eggs' rest.
A nest made of mud, leaves,
and twigs, and branches.
A nightingale needs a nice nest.

(Repeat first stanza.)
(Repeat second stanza.)
(Repeat first stanza.)
N.........no.

Track
15

Sing Along

"Oh, oh, oh, oh, no!"
said the ox. (Repeat)

"Not spots on my
awesome ostrich socks.
Not spots, not spots."
(Repeat)

(Repeat all)

Oo

TAXI

Pp

Sing Along

(Penguins) go prancing,
p......prancing. (Repeat)

Penguins and piglets,
peacocks prance.
Ponies and poodles,
it's how they all dance.

(Penguins) go prancing,
p......prance.

(Repeat lyrics above four
times, substituting piglets,
peacocks, ponies, and
poodles each round.)

Track
17

Qq

Sing Along

Queen Quail, Queen Quail, Queen Quail,
welcome to my quiz show.
(Repeat first line) I have a quiz for you.

Queen Quail, Queen Quail, Queen Quail,
I hear you have quadruplets.
(Repeat first line) I'll question you on them.

Queen Quail, Queen Quail, Queen Quail,
do your quadruplets quarrel?
(Repeat first line) or are they cute and quiet?

Queen Quail, Queen Quail, Queen Quail,
do your cute quadruplets quiver?
(Repeat first line) Do they quit under a quilt?

Queen Quail, Queen Quail, Queen Quail
I'll quit our quiz of questions.
(Repeat first line) Thank you for your quack!

Rr

Sing Along

Rufus is my red dog. He says,
"R.........ruff! R.........ruff!" (Repeat)

He ruffs at the rooster on the roof.
He says, "Ruff, ruff!"
He ruffs at the red roach on the road.
He says, "R.........ruff!"

Rufus is my red dog. He says,
"R.........ruff! R.........ruff!" (Repeat)

Sing Along

Essy, the snake, was sweet as a shake. She'd sing and she would smile. (Repeat)

Ss........ss.

Essy, the snake, was sweet as a shake. She'd sing and she would smile. (Repeat)

Ss

Sweets

Track 20

Sing Along

Tic-toc went the tired turtle's clock.
Tic-toc, tic-toc. (Repeat)

"I'm too tired to turn over," said the
tired turtle. "I'm terribly, terribly tired."

Tic-toc went the tired turtle's clock.
Tic-toc, tic-toc. (Repeat)

Sing Along

I understand umbrella birds
don't ever use umbrellas. (Repeat)
Up, up, up in the trees,
up, up up in the trees,
umbrella birds are usually happy.

I understand umbrella birds
don't ever use umbrellas. (Repeat)
Unless the unfortunate umbrella bird was
unlucky enough to get a short haircut.

Unfortunate umbrella birds, like
us, must use umbrellas. (Repeat)
But up, up, up in the trees,
up, up up in the trees,
umbrella birds are usually happy.

Vv

Sing Along

Victor, the vulture, is very, very nice.
(Repeat)

He isn't like most vultures; he eats
his vegetables. 'Cause Victor,
the vulture, is a vegetarian.
Victor, the vulture, is a vegetarian.

Track
23

Sing Along

Wiggly, wiggly, walrus
wiggly, wiggly, whee! (Repeat)

I wish I were a walrus.
I would be warm and wise.
I wish I were a walrus.
I would be ten times my size.

Wiggly, wiggly, walrus
wiggly, wiggly, whee! (Repeat)

I wish I were a walrus.
I'd wade in the warm, wet sea.
I wish I were a walrus. I'd wiggle.
Waves wouldn't catch me.

Wiggly, wiggly, walrus
wiggly, wiggly, whee! (Repeat)

Track
24

Xx

Sing Along

Roxie, the fox, found an x-ray box.
She heard, "x......"
It was heavy enough to be an ox.
She heard, "x......"

Roxie, the fox, was excited.
It must be an x-ray machine.
Roxie, the fox, found an x-ray box.
She heard, "x......"

Roxie, the fox, opened up the box.
She heard, "x......"
It wasn't an x-ray inside the box.
She heard, "x......"

But Roxie, the fox, was excited!
Though it wasn't an x-ray machine.
Roxie, the fox, had a fax machine
For all her fox faxing!

Yy

Sing Along

Yolanda, the yak, was a yodler.
"Yo-deh-leh-lay-hee-hoo!"
(Repeat)

She'd "Yo-duh-leh,
yo-deh-leh-lay-hee-hoo.
Yo-deh-leh-lay-hee-hoo!"

Yolanda, the yak, was a yodler.
"Yo-deh-leh-lay-hee-hoo!"
Yep!

Zz

ZOO ANIMAL EXCURSIONS

Sing Along

I'm Zina, the zebra, I zigzag
everywhere I go. (Repeat)

No circles for me like a zero. No
straight lines for me like a zippin'
zipper. No zeros or zippers for me.

I'm Zina, the zebra, I zigzag
everywhere I go. (Repeat)

No circles for me 'round the zoo. No
straight lines for me past the zookeeper,
too. No zeros or zippers for me.

I'm Zina, the zebra, I zigzag
everywhere I go. (Repeat)

I'm Zina, the zebra.
Some call me a zombie,
but that doesn't mean I won't zigzag.

Track
27

Karen